YA 921 MCN
Robinson, Tom.
Donovan McNabb

W9-COT-323

DATE DUE

SPORTS STARS WITH HEART
Donovan McNabb
LEADER ON AND OFF THE FIELD

by Tom Robinson

Enslow Publishers, Inc.
40 Industrial Road
Box 398
Berkeley Heights, NJ 07922
USA
http://www.enslow.com

Library of Congress Cataloging-in-Publication Data
Robinson, Tom.
  Donovan McNabb : leader on and off the field / by Tom Robinson.
    p. cm.—(Sports stars with heart)
  Includes bibliographical references and index.
  ISBN-13: 978-0-7660-2864-7
  ISBN-10: 0-7660-2864-X
  1. McNabb, Donovan—Juvenile literature. 2. Football players—United States—Biography—Juvenile literature. I. Title.

  GV939.M38R36 2007
  796.332092—dc22
    [B]   2006031841

Credits

Editorial Direction: Red Line Editorial, Inc. (Bob Temple)
Editor: Sue Green
Designer: The Design Lab

Printed in the United States of America

10 9 8 7 6 5 4 3 2 1

To Our Readers: We have done our best to make sure all Internet addresses in this book were active and appropriate when we went to press. However, the author and the publisher have no control over and assume no liability for the material available on those Internet sites or on other Web sites they may link to. Any comments or suggestions can be sent by e-mail to comments@enslow.com or to the address on the back cover.

Photographs © 2008: AP Photo/Elise Amendola: 69; AP Photo/Jim Barcus: 52; AP Photo/Stephen J. Boitano: 44; AP Photo/Tony Dejak: 1; AP Photo/Chris Gardner: 4, 7, 9; AP Photo/Morry Gash: 63; AP Photo/The Express-Times, Joe Gill: 46; AP Photo/Nam Y. Huh: 81; AP Photo/Joe Kaczmarek: 79; AP Photo/Miles Kennedy: 3, 76; AP Photo/Rusty Kennedy: 12, 49, 57, 84, 99, 104; AP Photo/Donna McWilliam: 92; AP Photo/Michael Okoniewski: 23; AP Photo/Gene J. Puskar: 87; AP Photo/Matt Rourke: 3, 101, 108; AP Photo/Amy Sancetta: 73; AP Photo/Paul Sancya: 18; AP Photo/Bill Sikes: 3, 28

Cover Photo: Donovan McNabb drops back to pass the ball in the Hall of Fame game August 6, 2006, in Canton, Ohio.

C O N T E N T S

Donovan McNabb grimaces in pain after hurting his ankle.

EAGLES

Playing Through the Pain

Donovan McNabb could always run the football better than just about every quarterback in the National Football League. McNabb was in the process of proving he could throw the ball and run an offense as effectively as the NFL's elite quarterbacks as well.

For the first time as a professional starter, McNabb did not run the ball at all for the Philadelphia Eagles in a game November 17, 2002. While making the 53rd start of his career, McNabb was simply a passer.

DONOVAN MCNABB

Team: Philadelphia Eagles

Position: Quarterback

Height: 6' 2"

Weight: 240

College: Syracuse

Birthdate: November 25, 1976

Hometown: Chicago, Ill.

All-Star: McNabb was named to play in the Pro Bowl five straight times, following the 2000–04 seasons.

DID YOU KNOW?

When Donovan McNabb ran for touchdowns in four straight games in the 2002 season, he became just the fifth NFL quarterback since 1970 to do so. The others were Greg Landry (1972), Pat Haden (1976), Jeff Hostetler (1993), and Kordell Stewart (1997).

There would be no scrambling from the pocket on this day, no rollouts on which he tucked the ball away and turned up the sideline, and no tricky bootlegs off fakes to running backs up the middle.

McNabb basically stood in one place and threw the football.

He had a reason. He was playing with a broken ankle. He adjusted.

McNabb suffered a broken ankle on the third play of a game against the Arizona Cardinals. He not only stayed in to pass the ball, he did it as well as ever, turning in perhaps the best passing day of his career. When he was done, he had completed 20 of 25 passes for 255 yards and 4 touchdowns. He led the Eagles to a 38–14 win against the Cardinals.

With the game done, McNabb could no longer hide the pain—or avoid the X-rays. The broken ankle was revealed, and McNabb had to miss six weeks, putting him on the sideline until the playoffs.

Putting together a career-best passing day while hobbling around with a broken bone is an extreme example, but McNabb has built a reputation throughout his career for playing through pain. The

Center Hank Fraley reaches down to injured quarterback Donovan McNabb during a 2002 game against Arizona.

toughness and ability that combined to produce the reputation led McNabb to hang on as long as possible in 2005 before finally having to concede that he was hurt too badly to play. After weeks of trying to play through pain, McNabb admitted that he needed surgery, this time ending his season early without the chance to return for the playoffs.

AN AMAZING NIGHT

As the Cardinals found out on that autumn day in 2002, it takes a lot to get McNabb off the football field.

An Arizona blitz worked on third-and-3, freeing up Adrian Wilson and LeVar Woods to sack McNabb and force a fumble. The Cardinals fell on the ball while the Eagles' offensive line circled around its fallen quarterback.

While the Cardinals had the ball, McNabb got ready to return. He was back for the next series and did not miss an offensive play until leaving the game with the Eagles well in front with 4:49 left to play. McNabb put the pain from his ankle out of his mind as much as possible.

"Donovan is a strong player. He's a warrior."

—Duce Staley

"I tried not to think about it," he said. "When the game was going on, I just focused on what I needed to do to get the win."[1]

There was work to do.

The fumble had led to an Arizona touchdown and early 7–0 lead.

By halftime, McNabb had his 4 touchdown passes, and the Eagles had a 28–14 lead. McNabb passed 2 yards to James Thrash in the first quarter and 3 yards to Dorsey Levens early in the second quarter for the first two scores. He lofted the ball down the left sideline to hit Todd Pinkston in stride for the 27-yard

McNabb smiles as the 2002 game with Arizona draws to an end.

score that broke a 14–14 tie in the second quarter. Duce Staley helped his quarterback by turning a screen pass into a 45-yard play on the next drive and then caught a 9-yard touchdown pass for the 14-point halftime lead.

Critics later wondered why McNabb was not done for the day after getting the Eagles the two-touchdown lead at halftime. Although he headed to the locker room for further examination as the defense finished out the first half, X-rays were never taken.

Even the toughest of football people would concede that it is not wise to play on a broken ankle. But McNabb was used to playing on sprains and other painful injuries and thought he was doing that again. His competitiveness kept him from realizing he was more seriously injured.

"Donovan was sure that he had sprained his ankle," Eagles coach Andy Reid said when he met with the media the next day. "It was similar to some ankle sprains he had before. Between Donovan's description and the examination of the medical staff, all signs pointed to a normal ankle sprain."[2]

BACK IN THE LINEUP

McNabb went to the sideline with the Eagles in first place. They boasted a 7–3 record, including 3–0 in games against NFC East Division opponents. His teammates held on from there, making the playoffs while waiting for McNabb's return.

AWARD WINNER

Some of the awards Donovan McNabb has received, on and off the field, include:

Big East Conference Offensive Player of the Decade for the 1990s.

USA Weekend Magazine's Most Caring Athletes (2003).

NFL Players' Association Perseverance Award (2004).

McNabb made it back in time to lead the Eagles to a 20–6 playoff victory against the Atlanta Falcons in the second week of January. Despite the injury, he got the Eagles to the National Football Conference (NFC) Championship game.

The Eagles had their season end with a loss in the NFC title game for the second of three straight times.

With McNabb leading the way, the Eagles remained among the league's top four teams for four seasons. They finally reached the Super Bowl following the 2004 season only to lose, 24–21, to the New England Patriots, who were wrapping up their third championship in four seasons.

TROUBLESOME SEASON

By the time the 2005 season arrived, it was clear that the Eagles could count on McNabb to lead the way. Earlier experience had also made it clear that he was tough to stop even when not at 100 percent physically.

McNabb entered the season with some soreness in his abdomen. As the Eagles made it through the first month of the season, McNabb also had a bruised chest and a shin contusion.

While he was beat up physically, McNabb was picking apart opponents. He threw for 342 yards and 5 touchdowns in just three quarters against the San Francisco 49ers. Then, the Eagles called on him to throw 52 passes for 365 yards against the Oakland Raiders.

McNabb suffered an abdominal strain during the demanding game against Oakland. Further examination identified the injury as a sports hernia, an injury that would probably require surgery to repair.

The injury left McNabb uncomfortable, but he chose to play anyway.

McNabb passes during the second half of a 2005 game against the San Francisco 49ers.

"We're hoping it's something we'll be able to manage," Eagles trainer Rick Burkholder said at the time.[3]

Reid decided to watch how McNabb played with the injury.

"If it ends up where he can't function, then we'll shut him down," Reid said.[4]

Just a day after the diagnosis, McNabb made it clear how he wanted to proceed. Immediate surgery was not a consideration.

"I'm ready to go," McNabb said. "I don't have any concerns right now. It's just something that you have to deal with and realize some days you'll feel great and some days you won't."[5]

As if to prove he was not ready to give up, McNabb passed for 369 yards and 3 touchdowns while leading a come-from-behind, 37–31 victory in Kansas City later that week.

Even in pain, McNabb performed well enough to be named the NFC's Offensive Player of the Month for September.

> **"I don't have any concerns right now. It's just something that you have to deal with and realize some days you'll feel great and some days you won't."**
>
> **—Donovan McNabb**

13

He could not, however, maintain the pace. With little support from a Philadelphia running attack that was struggling, McNabb was called on to throw 45 or more passes four times. The tear in his abdomen meant he could no longer avoid pass rushes the way he used to, which led to even more hits to his bruised and battered body.

HIGHEST WINNING PERCENTAGE AMONG ACTIVE QUARTERBACKS (MINIMUM 80 STARTS) (THROUGH END OF 2005 SEASON)		
Donovan McNabb	60–28	.682
Brett Favre	139–82	.629
Peyton Manning	80–48	.625
Brad Johnson	65–43	.602
Steve McNair	76–56	.576

McNabb's production eventually fell off, and the Eagles started losing consistently for the first time since he took over as their starting quarterback. Even with the late slip, when the season ended, the Eagles were 60–28 in career games started by McNabb. He had the best winning percentage of any active quarterback in the NFL.

When McNabb threw an interception late in a game against Dallas, he aggravated his groin, which was feeling the effects of the sports hernia. He missed a tackle and watched Roy Williams return the interception for a touchdown and a Cowboys victory. The loss was the third of four straight for Philadelphia.

McNabb sat out the next game. Then, he finally made the difficult decision.

This was another injury that McNabb could no longer play through. With what he had accomplished in his career while hurting, how could McNabb not have been expected to do it again? How could he not expect that of himself? Eventually, however, it became clear that he was beginning to hurt the team and perhaps his chances of helping the team in the future.

"Once the groin becomes an issue, then the recovery is not going to take place and rest is not going to help it," Reid said. "It is just too much discomfort to where Donovan can't run and function."[6]

McNabb made the announcement the week before Thanksgiving that he would have the surgery and end his season early.

PHILADELPHIA EAGLES' RECORD (DURING DONOVAN MCNABB'S CAREER)

Year	W–L
1999	5–11
2000	11–5
2001	11–5
2002	12–4
2003	12–4
2004	13–3
2005	6–10

"I'm disappointed that the injury has reached this stage and has ultimately ended my season. I wanted so much to help this team turn it around and was unable to do that."

—Donovan McNabb

"I'm disappointed that the injury has reached this stage and has ultimately ended my season," McNabb said in a statement that day. "I wanted so much to help this team turn it around and was unable to do that."[7]

After four straight seasons that ended in either the Super Bowl or NFC Championship game, the Eagles finished with a losing record.

McNabb went through with surgery and came back to quarterback the Eagles again in 2006. Once and for all, he proved that he was the team's true leader.

CHAPTER TWO

Young Donovan

Donovan McNabb remembers what it was like to be a young fan.

Before Donovan was ever on the cover of *Sports Illustrated*, he admired the photos of the athletes who made appearances there. Many of the covers wound up on the walls in his room.

Like most adults, much of what Donovan is about today can be traced to his childhood.

Donovan's mother, Wilma, was a nurse. His grandmother died from complications of diabetes, and eventually his father, Sam, struggled with the disease. When Donovan decided to use some of his fame and fortune to be heavily involved in charities later in life, it was no surprise that the American Diabetes Association would become one of the top beneficiaries.

Donovan McNabb and Jerome Bettis are close to their mothers.

Donovan grew up in the Chicago suburb of Dolton and looked up to professional athletes. He was also surrounded by younger and less-established athletes. He followed the play of his older brother. In high school, Donovan also played alongside future professional all-stars Simeon Rice in football and Antoine Walker in basketball.

One of the things that makes Donovan unique is that he can mix the serious leadership demanded of the quarterback position with laughter. That, too, is a trait developed in his childhood.

MOUNT CARMEL GRADUATES IN THE NFL (DURING 2005 SEASON)

Matt Cushing
Steve Edwards
Donovan McNabb
Simeon Rice
Derrick Strong

Donovan started playing Pee Wee football in fourth grade. Wilma McNabb remembers teachers and her son's early coaches telling her that Donovan was a clown. He always seemed to be joking around, and they did not know if he was capable of being serious.

"We'd say to him, 'Why can't you be serious? What do you want to be, a comedian?'" Wilma McNabb said.[1]

Sam and Wilma saw their son get good grades. They saw his early accomplishments on the playing fields. They decided not to worry.

FOOTBALL POWERS

By the time Donovan McNabb ended his freshman football season in high school, he had already been part of an undefeated state championship team.

Mount Carmel High School fought through 3 straight wins by 7 or fewer points before shutting out Wheaton Central, 24–0, in the 1990 Illinois Class 5A state football championship game. Mount Carmel shook off two regular-season losses during the 1991 season to win its fourth straight 5A championship. After winning 3 straight playoff shutouts by at least 27 points, Mount Carmel defeated Rockford Boylan, 28–6, in the semifinals, then Wheaton Central, 21–14, in the championship game rematch.

During Donovan's four years of high school, Mount Carmel went 49–5 with two of the losses coming in the state playoffs. Joliet Catholic eliminated Mount Carmel, 13–11, in the 1992 state semifinal that matched the two most successful programs in Illinois high school history.

Mount Carmel lost to Chicago rival De La Salle, 9–6, in a 1993 state playoff game that ended Donovan's high school career.

Donovan wound up at Mount Carmel, an all-male high school on the south side of the city. It boasted one of the top athletic programs in Chicago. The same questions came up there during basketball.

"That's Donovan's way," Wilma said. "He wants to have fun. He told me, 'Mom, if I can't have fun doing something, what's the point of doing it?'"[2]

Donovan excelled on the basketball court as a two-time all-star, but he was at his best during the football season. The *Chicago Defender News* named Donovan Player of the Year. He also earned recognition as an All-American at the program that has produced nine state titles under coach Frank Lenti.

"When we first saw Donovan, you knew he was something special," said assistant coach David Lenti, Frank's younger brother. "He's very charismatic, an outstanding young man; so much character, so much class."[3]

Donovan kept his playful style through college, and it is still part of his game in the NFL.

"I just enjoy playing," Donovan said. "I love the competition. People say, 'I was watching the game, and it looked like you were smiling out there.' Yeah, I probably was. I love that feeling, everyone in the huddle looking at me, eyes wide. It's like, 'This is it. Who wants to make the big play?' I love having the ball in my hands in that situation. That's just me.

"Like when people talk about me joking around. I always did that. I did it in high school, I did it in Syracuse, and so I kept doing it when I came here."[4]

MOUNT CARMEL STATE TITLES

Year – Classification
1980 – 5A
1988 – 6A
1989 – 5A
1990 – 5A
1991 – 5A
1996 – 5A
1998 – 5A
1999 – 4A
2000 – 5A
2002 – 6A

McNabb clowns on the sidelines of a Syracuse game.

MOVING ON

Donovan made some lists of the nation's top high school football players, but his status as a recruit was uncertain. Not many schools saw him as a Division I-A quarterback. He was unwanted in the Big Ten, where many Chicago-area high school stars aspired to play.

Although his athletic ability was often recognized, Donovan's passing numbers were limited in high school. As a senior, he passed for 874 yards and 12 touchdowns and rushed for 633 yards and 13 more scores. Some stereotypical questions were raised. Before Donovan, Michael Vick, and Daunte Culpepper, there were still coaches who were hesitant to rely on African-American quarterbacks, particularly those they did not picture as traditional drop-back passers.

"Why wouldn't a school want a black quarterback?" Wilma McNabb asked. "Maybe in their minds, we weren't qualified to be there."[5]

Nebraska offered Donovan a chance to play quarterback in its option offense, which stressed running by the quarterback. Syracuse coach Paul Pasqualoni also saw something he liked.

DID YOU KNOW?

Donovan McNabb started the Donovan McNabb Golden Arm Scholarship. The scholarships, which are for students at Mount Carmel High School with grade-point averages of 2.5 or better, are awarded based on essays the students write about their lives.

"Tell me who recruited Donovan McNabb. Syracuse and Nebraska."

—Paul Pasqualoni

"Tell me who recruited Donovan McNabb," Pasqualoni said years later. "Syracuse and Nebraska.

"Did anybody in the Big Ten offer Donovan McNabb a scholarship? No."[6]

The lack of offers did not matter. Donovan accepted Syracuse's offer of a full football scholarship and soon found himself at home there.

CHAPTER THREE

Two-Sport Star at Syracuse

Donovan McNabb made the most of his time at Syracuse. But first he had to wait. McNabb sat through a redshirt season in 1994, before becoming an active part of the football program in 1995.

Even as the 1995 season was about to open, McNabb had to wait. He was in competition with Kevin Mason and Kevin Johnson for the starting quarterback job throughout preseason practice in the summer. Coach Paul Pasqualoni kept an eye on the candidates for the job, but he kept his opinions to himself. Pasqualoni finally declared the starting quarterback just hours before the season opener. He let McNabb claim the important position of leading the Orangemen on offense.

McNabb immediately made his coach look wise for trusting a redshirt freshman. The offense had its share of struggles for the first three quarters in the opener. Then, McNabb guided three fourth-quarter touchdown drives in an impressive 20–9 victory against North Carolina.

There was never any more doubt as to who would start at quarterback for the Orangemen. McNabb held the position for all 45 games of his college football career, taking Syracuse to four straight bowl games and a 33–12 record through the completion of his career at the end of the 1998 season.

"He was a sponge," Pasqualoni said. "Anything you could show him to help him, he would soak up and be thirsty for more."[1]

> **DID YOU KNOW?**
> Syracuse University went to four different bowl games in Donovan McNabb's four seasons as quarterback. After going to the Gator Bowl at the end of McNabb's freshman season, the Orangemen headed to the Liberty Bowl, Fiesta Bowl, and Orange Bowl. They beat Houston, 30–16, when McNabb was a sophomore. They lost to Kansas State, 35–17, in the Fiesta Bowl and then to Florida, 31–10, in the Orange Bowl.

The fourth-quarter rally against North Carolina was just the start of the excitement McNabb would bring to the Syracuse offense with his combination of passing and running. He threw for 2,300 yards as a freshman, including an electrifying 96-yard touchdown pass to Marvin Harrison against West Virginia. He also

McNabb throws a pass against Virginia Tech.

ran for 526 yards, establishing his trend of putting up high numbers on the ground when compared to other quarterbacks.

McNabb's freshman season actually finished on New Year's Day 1996, because he led Syracuse to an appearance in the Gator Bowl in Jacksonville, Florida. McNabb started the new year in style. He ran 5 yards for a touchdown and passed 38 yards to Harrison for another to get Syracuse out to a 20–0 lead against Clemson before the first quarter was complete.

When his first bowl game was done, McNabb had completed 13 of 23 passes for 309 yards. He threw two more touchdowns—a 56-yarder to Harrison and a 15-yarder to Kaseen Sinceno—in the 41–0 rout. As a result, McNabb was named Most Valuable Player.

Just one year into his college football career, McNabb was collecting awards. He was also named Rookie of the Year in the Big East Conference.

KEEPING BUSY

The days of playing multiple sports end for most athletes when they accept a full scholarship to play in college.

McNabb was an exception. He accepted a scholarship to Syracuse University to play football and did it about as well as anyone in the history of the Big East Conference.

That was not all.

There were two main reasons why he chose Syracuse instead of Nebraska. McNabb knew he would get to pass and not just be labeled a running quarterback in Nebraska's option offense, which does not prepare many quarterbacks for possible professional careers. In addition, Pasqualoni did not rule out the possibility of McNabb continuing with basketball once his football commitments were fulfilled.

McNabb was busy during his days playing in the Carrier Dome. He set many Big East football records that still stand. He also served as a backup guard on the Orange basketball team for two seasons, including one that resulted in a trip to the Final Four. In addition, he earned a degree in speech communications and minored in African-American studies. It was just the beginning of a long relationship with

RECORD-SETTER

College football records set by Donovan McNabb while playing at Syracuse from 1995 to 1998:

BIG EAST RECORDS

Career Passing Yards – 8,389

Career Touchdown Passes – 77

Career Total Offensive Yards– 9,950

Career Total Touchdowns – 96

SCHOOL RECORDS

Career Touchdown Passes – 77

Career Total Offensive Yards– 9,950

Career Total Touchdowns – 96

Career Passing Efficiency – 155.1

Season Touchdown Passes – 22

Season Total Offensive Yards – 2,892

Syracuse University. McNabb is the youngest person ever elected to the Board of Trustees at Syracuse, where he has made some major financial contributions.

LATE START

While the rest of the basketball team got together for preseason practices and the start of non-league games, McNabb was occupied elsewhere. He was still playing quarterback on the school's football team.

Despite the late start, McNabb found ways to contribute to the basketball program in the two years that he served as a backup guard. He joined the 1995–96 team in progress for its run all the way to the national championship game, which it lost to Kentucky, 76–67. Antoine Walker, McNabb's former high school teammate, scored 11 points for Kentucky in the championship game.

McNabb played just 11 minutes in three games, but he was a key fill-in for one of the team's biggest wins of the season. McNabb came off the bench to play 8 minutes, making him the third-busiest substitute in the NCAA Tournament Sweet 16 game. Syracuse trailed, 52–42, in the second half before rallying to force a 70–70 tie with Georgia at the end of regulation. John Wallace, who led the 83–81 win with 30 points and 15 rebounds, hit a three-pointer with two seconds left in overtime to complete another comeback.

The Orangemen were one win away from the Final Four. They added two wins to finish 29–9 and in second place in the country.

McNabb eventually gave up basketball to prepare for his pro football career, but not until after he played another partial season with the Orangemen. He was a bigger part of the team as a sophomore, averaging 2.8 points, 1.3 rebounds, and 0.5 assists while playing for coach Jim Boeheim in one of the nation's top programs. Into his pro football career, McNabb continued to excel on the basketball court in pickup and charity basketball games.

McNabb also met his future wife through Syracuse basketball. Racquel "Roxi" Nurse was a four-year starter on the women's basketball team while McNabb was still in school.

ALL-DECADE

Syracuse players on the Big East's all-decade team for the 1990s:

Offensive Player of the Decade – Donovan McNabb

Special Teams Player of the Decade – Kevin Johnson

Quarterback – Donovan McNabb

Wide Receiver – Marvin Harrison

Kickoff Returner – Kevin Johnson

Cornerback – Kevin Abrams

Safety – Donovin Darius

MORE TO ACCOMPLISH

While McNabb's basketball career was winding down, his college football career was just getting started.

McNabb followed up his Rookie of the Year performance in 1995 by earning Big East Offensive Player of the Year honors in each of his three remaining seasons. He is the conference's only three-time Offensive Player of the Year. He also was the first player ever named first-team Big East all-star for four straight seasons.

With McNabb leading the way, Syracuse caught defending champion Miami and shared the Big East title in his sophomore year. The Orangemen won the title outright in 1997 and 1998.

When the Big East decided to mark the first ten years of its football conference, it selected an All-Decade team for the 1990s. McNabb was named Offensive Player of the Decade in the conference.

The Orangemen opened the 1997 season with a 34–0 win against Wisconsin in the Kickoff Classic. After a surprising slip to three straight losses, they won 8 straight and the Big East championship.

Syracuse was even considered a possible national title contender during McNabb's senior year. Those hopes, however, were seriously damaged in a controversial 34–33 loss to Tennessee in the season opener, despite 300 passing yards by McNabb. Tennessee went on to win the national championship.

DID YOU KNOW?

Donovan McNabb had three of the top four seasons in Syracuse University history in passing-efficiency rating. All four of his seasons rank in the top ten in school history. Players needed a minimum of 100 passing attempts in a season to be considered. A 100.0 rating is considered average in the NCAA formula.

Place	Player	Year	Rating
1	Don McPherson	1987	164.3
2	Donovan McNabb	1995	162.3
3	Donovan McNabb	1998	158.9
4	Donovan McNabb	1997	154.0
5	Bill Scharr	1989	152.2
6	Don McPherson	1985	149.8
7	Marvin Graves	1992	149.2
8	Todd Philcox	1988	147.9
9	Marvin Graves	1993	147.3
10	Donovan McNabb	1996	145.1

Syracuse showed it was able to come back from the tough loss by beating defending national champion Michigan, 38–28, in the next game.

1998 HEISMAN TROPHY VOTING

Place	Player	School	Year	Position	First-place Votes	Voting Points
1	Ricky Williams	Texas	Senior	Running back	714	2,355
2	Michael Bishop	Kansas State	Senior	Quarterback	41	792
3	Cade McNown	UCLA	Senior	Quarterback	28	696
4	Tim Couch	Kentucky	Junior	Quarterback	26	527
5	Donovan McNabb	Syracuse	Senior	Quarterback	13	232
6	Daunte Culpepper	Central Florida	Senior	Quarterback	5	67
7	Champ Bailey	Georgia	Senior	Defensive Back	6	55
8	Torry Holt	North Carolina State	Senior	Wide Receiver	2	44
9	Joe Germaine	Ohio State	Senior	Quarterback	2	43
10	Shaun King	Tulane	Senior	Quarterback	1	38

The Orangemen had dramatic wins before the year was done. McNabb hit Stephen Brominski with a 14-yard touchdown pass on the final play of the game in a 28–26 victory against Virginia Tech. McNabb spiked the ball with five seconds left, stopping the clock and setting up the play that completed a rally from a 21–6 deficit.

Syracuse had never beaten Miami in football before McNabb arrived. After losing a chance at sole possession of a title by falling to the Hurricanes in

McNabb's sophomore year, the Orangemen beat Miami twice in a row. The second win was a 66–13 rout in McNabb's final game at the Carrier Dome.

With his Syracuse career coming to a close, McNabb finished fifth in the balloting for the Heisman Trophy award, the most prestigious honor in college football.

In the end, Pasqualoni was happy he took a chance on a player who was not exactly overwhelmed with college opportunities. He frequently mentioned McNabb as an example of why the coaching staff had to trust its own knowledge and not follow the ideas of various scouting groups that attempt to rank college football prospects.

"It is our job to identify prospects. It is our job to evaluate them," Pasqualoni said. He added that he was not nervous about offering scholarships to players who were not on recruiting lists. "If that was the case, we would never have signed Donovan McNabb."[2]

FAMOUS SYRACUSE FOOTBALL PLAYERS

Jim Brown

Ernie Davis

John Mackey

Floyd Little

Larry Csonka

Art Monk

Donovan McNabb

LASTING LEGACY

McNabb's connection to Syracuse University went beyond joining the impressive list of football greats the school has produced.

A reading program that connected the school's athletes

> **"There is not a better role model for any athlete in the country than Donovan McNabb. Thank you, Donovan."**
>
> **—Daryl Gross**

with elementary students around the Syracuse area has greatly expanded in the time since McNabb helped get it started.

McNabb's financial contributions have helped the athletic department improve its facilities and keep attracting some of the nation's top high school athletes to the winter wonderland in upstate New York.

Syracuse athletics director Daryl Gross publicly thanked McNabb at the groundbreaking ceremony for a training facility that McNabb played a major role in helping to finance.

"Donovan, we are so appreciative to you and Roxi for giving back to your school," Gross said. "He did it on the field. He did it academically.

"He's a Board of Trustee member for us. Super Bowl. Pro Bowl. Off the field. Community. There is not a better role model for any athlete in the country than Donovan McNabb. Thank you, Donovan."[3]

CHAPTER FOUR

Draft Day Questions

NFL commissioner Paul Tagliabue stepped to the microphone. He was about to make a dream come true for Donovan McNabb. Angelo Cataldi, a sports talk radio host at WIP-610 in Philadelphia, had already used his microphone to try to turn April 18, 1999, into a nightmare for McNabb.

Word had come out of the Philadelphia Eagles' front office that the team planned on using the second pick in the NFL Draft to make McNabb the franchise's next quarterback. Cataldi disagreed with the plan and used his radio show to try to convince the Eagles that they should take Heisman Trophy winner Ricky Williams, who had set college rushing records at the University of Texas.

Even Philadelphia mayor Ed Rendell weighed in, agreeing with Cataldi that the Eagles should pick Williams. Cataldi organized a group of about thirty fans to drive to New York on draft day. When they arrived at Madison Square Garden, the fans began chanting for the selection of Williams.

When Tagliabue made it official, announcing that the Eagles had used their second pick to select McNabb, the group of fans loudly booed the announcement. Hindsight shows that the Eagles

1999 NFL DRAFT
TOP 10 PICKS

Pick	NFL Team	Player	Position	College
1	Cleveland Browns	Tim Couch	Quarterback	Kentucky
2	Philadelphia Eagles	Donovan McNabb	Quarterback	Syracuse
3	Cincinnati Bengals	Akili Smith	Quarterback	Oregon
4	Indianapolis Colts	Edgerrin James	Running Back	Miami, Florida
5	New Orleans Saints	Ricky Williams	Running Back	Texas
6	St. Louis Rams	Torry Holt	Wide Receiver	North Carolina State
7	Washington Redskins	Champ Bailey	Defensive Back	Georgia
8	Arizona Cardinals	David Boston	Wide Receiver	Ohio State
9	Detroit Lions	Chris Claiborne	Linebacker	Louisiana State
10	Baltimore Ravens	Chris McAlister	Defensive Back	Arizona

made a wise selection. They added a Pro Bowl quarterback and avoided the problems that eventually plagued Williams when issues involving drug use sidetracked his career.

On that day in New York, however, it was hard to tell if McNabb and the Eagles were meant for each other. Wilma McNabb cried. Bewildered, Sam McNabb asked his son what was happening.

"Just think about it," Eagles president Joe Banner said. "That moment, of walking on stage with NFL commissioner Paul Tagliabue, is a dream he'd had his whole life and it wasn't what he pictured."[1]

McNabb reassured his parents and, in his actions, assured the Eagles that new head coach Andy Reid was correct in thinking McNabb was the right man to lead their team.

"Andy had a long list of reasons why he liked Donovan and at the top was his belief that Donovan could handle being in a town that was tough on you," Banner said. "We just never knew his mettle would be tested so quickly.

"I think that day, Donovan realized the nature of our city."[2]

The passion that Philadelphians show for football is something that McNabb has come to appreciate. "You just know that people love their football across the Philadelphia area and Pennsylvania," McNabb said. "They're counting down to opening kickoff and

"Andy had a long list of reasons why he liked Donovan and at the top was his belief that Donovan could handle being in a town that was tough on you."

—Joe Banner

are ready to go. As a player, that gives you added motivation."[3]

Not all of Philadelphia was against choosing McNabb. The vocal group at the draft, however, made that the first impression.

McNabb was intent on not jumping to conclusions about the difficulty he faced trying to win over Philadelphia fans.

"All we have to do really is to get everything back to the way it used to be, get back on the winning track, then they'll believe it was the right pick," McNabb said.[4]

Still, the reception that his selection received did serve as motivation.

"They're pointing and booing," McNabb said in an interview for the Fox Sports Net series *Beyond the Glory*. The reaction got to him "to the point that my motivation was so high, I couldn't wait to get started."[5]

**QUARTERBACKS PICKED
IN 1999 DRAFT**

Tim Couch, Cleveland

Donovan McNabb,
     Philadelphia

Akili Smith, Cincinnati

Daunte Culpepper, Minnesota

Cade McNown, Chicago

Shaun King, Tampa Bay

Brock Huard, Seattle

Joe Germaine, St. Louis

Aaron Brooks, Green Bay

Kevin Daft, Tennessee

Michael Bishop,
     New England

Chris Greisen, Arizona

Scott Covington,
     Cincinnati

The questions were not new to McNabb. Out of high school, only two major college football programs wanted him as their quarterback. Now, at least one group of fans for his professional team made it clear that they did not want the college star.

"Donovan was Donovan, he didn't show it," Banner said. "But, frankly, he's human, and I can't say it didn't affect him at all."[6]

With Philadelphia's well-earned reputation for having fans who can be tough on even the hometown players, McNabb had some challenges ahead.

As he embarked on his professional career, McNabb would be compared with Williams. Running backs traditionally have a less difficult transition from the college to the pro game, so Williams figured to be an immediate factor in the NFL. There would also be comparisons with other quarterbacks from a strong group that entered the league together in the 1999 Draft.

DRAFT ANTICIPATION

Just as high school football prospects are ranked by various scouting services, analysis of the NFL Draft is done in advance. The intensity of the debate, however, is much stronger because players are now gaining fame from their college careers, and no other sport in the United States is followed with the same passion as the NFL is.

For all the debate and "draft experts," teams make their choices based on their own observations and the executives and coaches who are paid to make those decisions.

As the draft approached, McNabb was receiving extra attention and follow-up interviews from some teams, including the Eagles.

"These second interviews are a lot more personal—teams want to find out more on the mental side of things," McNabb wrote in a draft diary for *Sports Illustrated*. "I've tried to convey to them that I'm just excited about the opportunity to be a team's top pick, to be part of a team."[7]

McNabb tried asking his own questions during the evaluation process.

"I still need some answers myself," he wrote. "What are their goals? What is their outlook for next year? How would drafting Donovan McNabb change their offense?

"I want to see if they're excited about me."[8]

McNabb jumps over teammate Jermane Mayberry.

McNabb knew there were key differences in this process from when he chose a college. The most significant was that, in this case, the team would be selecting him.

"Out of high school, you have a chance to choose the team that you and your parents think is best for you," he said. "Now, it's out of your hands."[9]

DRAFT ANALYSIS

Although it is out of the hands of fans, writers, and broadcasters, those groups tend to want to do their share of projecting what is best. Only Daunte Culpepper went on to have a comparable career from that highly regarded draft class of quarterbacks, but a *Sports Illustrated* poll showed that readers expected more from other quarterbacks.

CNNSI.COM POLL, 1999 DRAFT WHICH QB WILL HAVE THE MOST SUCCESSFUL CAREER IN THE NFL?	
Tim Couch	27%
Cade McNown	23%
Donovan McNabb	19%
Daunte Culpepper	15%
Akili Smith	13%
Brock Huard	3%
(4,527 Internet votes)	

When the NFL teams made their choices, they picked quarterbacks with the first three spots. It was the first time that had happened in twenty-eight years. A total of five quarterbacks went in the top twelve picks.

McNabb is chased out of the pocket by defensive tackle Kelly Gregg during a full-contact drill at training camp in 2000.

GOING CAMPING

Regardless of whether it was a popular choice, McNabb was now a member of the Philadelphia Eagles. His first training camp with the team would be a chance to begin winning over the remaining fans, and more important, prove to Reid and his staff that he was the right choice.

PHILADELPHIA EAGLES' 1999 DRAFT PICKS

Round	Overall Pick	Player	Position	College
1	2	Donovan McNabb	Quarterback	Syracuse
2	35	Barry Gardner	Inside linebacker	Northwestern
3	64	Doug Brzezinski	Guard	Boston College
4	97	John Welbourn	Guard	California
4	128	Damon Moore	Defensive Back	Ohio State
4	130	Na Brown	Wide Receiver	North Carolina
6	172	Cecil Martin	Fullback	Wisconsin
6	201	Troy Smith	Wide Receiver	East Carolina
7	208	Jed Weaver	Tight End	Oregon
7	251	Pernell Davis	Defensive Tackle	Alabama-Birmingham

Safety Tim Hauck, a veteran on that first team, said it did not take McNabb long to make a positive impression. Hauck had been with the Indianapolis Colts a year earlier and was able to observe the debut of another big-time quarterback—Peyton Manning.

"I knew Donovan would be special because I played with the Colts when Peyton was a rookie," Hauck said. "That year, Manning was thrown to the wolves, leading the league in interceptions. Both rookies had great size, and a calm pocket presence. And McNabb's ability to elude tacklers as a rookie in practice jumped out at me."[10]

Taking Over in Philadelphia

cNabb entered the NFL in 1999 trying to prove he was capable of running the Philadelphia Eagles' offense effectively. By the time the 2000 season was done, there was no question whether McNabb could perform as a quarterback in the NFL. The question had become whether he was being required to do too much for the Eagles.

McNabb needed a game to make an impact at Syracuse University. By the end of the first season, he had clearly taken over as the future of the school's football program. The process took a little longer in Philadelphia. McNabb played in most of the games and started nearly half of them in his rookie season. Although he was an immediate threat as a running quarterback, he hit fewer than half his passes during that rookie season.

The 2000 season was drastically different. It was a reversal of fortunes for the Eagles, who went from 5–11 the year before to 11–5. McNabb finished as runner-up in voting for the NFL's Most Valuable Player award, behind only Marshall Faulk of the St. Louis Rams. Faulk had set the NFL record for most touchdowns in a season. McNabb finished the season by making his Pro Bowl debut and leading the National Football Conference to a touchdown on his first drive in the all-star game.

McNabb escapes the Cardinals' defense.

A LITTLE OF EVERYTHING

McNabb was named NFC Offensive Player of the Week twice during the 2000 season. He was honored following a 23–20 win against the Washington Redskins after rushing for 125 yards, the most by an NFL quarterback in twenty-eight years. Two weeks later, McNabb passed for what was then his career high of 390 yards and 4 touchdowns in a win against the Cleveland Browns to earn the honor again.

Injuries to other offensive players did not matter. McNabb passed for 3,365 yards and ran for 629. He accounted for an astounding 75 percent of the yardage gained by the Eagles. Coach Andy Reid was frequently asked whether that number was too high.

"I don't mess with that stuff," Reid said. "Obviously, you want to spread it around and become more balanced. . . . You're going to do whatever it

MOST YARDS RUSHING IN A SEASON BY AN NFL QUARTERBACK		
Michael Vick, Atlanta,	2006	1,039
Randall Cunningham, Philadelphia	1990	942
Michael Vick, Atlanta	2004	902
Michael Vick, Atlanta	2002	777
Steve McNair, Tennessee	1997	674
Donovan McNabb, Philadelphia	2000	629

takes to win. However the percentages come out, they come out. But I guess if you looked at that percentage, you'd say you'd like to spread it around a little more."[1]

McNabb's rushing numbers were among the best ever produced by an NFL quarterback. "I never got the feeling like he was trying to do too much," Reid said. "If it's not there, and you have to go, you go. I'm never going to tell him to stop running. I'm not going to tell him, 'You run too much,' because he has a great feel for the offense. He's very patient with it and lets things happen."[2]

MAKING HIS DEBUT

When McNabb reported to his first professional camp, he already had the idea that he was going in to compete for a starting job. "I'm confident in myself that I can learn the offense and step in there and do what I've been able to do throughout college," he said. "I don't believe in sitting on the bench. I'm not going to work to sit on the bench. I'm going to work to be the starter. If I'm rewarded with the starting position, I'm going to work for higher goals."[3]

Before long, McNabb was progressing toward the first goal. He came off the bench September 19, 1999, to play in the second half of a 19–5 loss to the Tampa Bay Buccaneers. He ran well, gaining 38 yards on 5 carries, but he hit just 4 of 11 passes for 26 yards.

McNabbs gets by the Chiefs' Norris McCleary in the third quarter of a November 29, 2001, game in Kansas City.

Reid put McNabb in late in five other games before turning the starting assignment over to his rookie quarterback on November 14. Still searching for the feel of the passing game against NFL defenses,

McNabb found a way to lead the team to a 35–28 victory. The Eagles trailed, 21–10, into the final minute of the first half, but they scored the winning touchdown on an 11-yard Eric Bienemy run with less than four minutes left. McNabb passed for just 60 yards, but he ran for 49. He passed for one two-point conversion and ran for another.

A week later, McNabb threw his first NFL touchdown pass, a 6-yarder to Chad Lewis during a 44–17 loss to the Indianapolis Colts.

McNabb started 6 of the final 7 games for the season. He threw for 3 touchdowns in the season finale, a 38–31 victory against the St. Louis Rams.

The Eagles finished just 5–11, but starting safety Tim Hauck, who played fourteen years in the NFL, saw positive signs. "We had a solid defense and when Donovan McNabb got his chance to play as a rookie, he made some things happen," Hauck said. "So, as a team, we felt we were in much better shape than our record indicated."[4]

PROGRESSING QUICKLY

The progress started showing early in the 2000 season. The Eagles were 2–2 and off to a respectable start when McNabb, who would start every game of the season, made his NFL prime-time debut on ESPN. McNabb had his first 300-yard passing game as a pro. He went 30-for-44 for 311 yards as the

FASTEST NFL QUARTERBACKS TO 50 WINS

Ken Stabler	62 career starts
Tom Brady	65 career starts
Danny White	69 career starts
Jim McMahon	70 career starts
Donovan McNabb	71 career starts

2000 NFC PLAYOFFS

Wild-Card

New Orleans 31, St. Louis 28

Philadelphia 21, Tampa Bay 3

Divisional

Minnesota 34, New Orleans 16

New York Giants 20, Philadelphia 10

NFC Championship

New York Giants 41, Minnesota 0

Note: Baltimore 34, New York Giants 7 in Super Bowl

Eagles blew out the Atlanta Falcons in a 38–10 romp.

The Eagles became a playoff contender with four straight wins in November, starting with overtime wins against the Dallas Cowboys and Pittsburgh Steelers. They trailed the Steelers by 10 points with 2 minutes left in regulation. After a comfortable win over Arizona, the Eagles pulled out a three-point win over Washington to improve to 9–4.

McNabb brought the Eagles from behind in the third quarter when he outran Bruce Smith, faked his way past Mark Carrier, and then dragged Matt Stevens with him into the end zone for a 21-yard touchdown. He later raced 54 yards to set up the game-winning field goal.

PLAYOFF TEAM

The Eagles finished their 11–5 regular season with two straight wins. They headed for the playoffs behind their quarterback, who set team records for passing attempts (569) and completions (330) in a season.

McNabb ran for a touchdown and passed for another in the last three minutes of the first half to give the Eagles a 14–3 lead against the Tampa Bay Buccaneers in the wild-card playoff game. He protected the lead with a safe, short passing game, completing 24 of 33 attempts in the 21–3 triumph.

The division rival New York Giants ended the Eagles' season a week later. The Giants returned the opening kickoff and then an interception for touchdowns in a 20–10 victory. McNabb's first full season as a starter was done, but he was already being considered among the most valuable players in the NFL.

DONOVAN MCNABB'S 2000 PLAYOFF STATISTICS

vs. Tampa Bay: 24-for-33, 161 yards, 2 TDs, 1 interception; 8-for-32, 1 TD rushing

vs. New York Giants: 20-for-41, 181 yards, 1 TD, 1 interception; 5-for-17 rushing

CHAPTER SIX

Knocking on the Door

The Philadelphia Eagles trailed the Green Bay Packers, 14–0, early in their National Football Conference divisional playoff game January 11, 2004, but they came back. Donovan McNabb was sacked 8 times, but he kept getting back up.

When the Eagles faced a three-point deficit and a fourth-and-26 situation with 1:12 remaining, it seemed they had finally run out of ways to respond. McNabb and receiver Freddie Mitchell made sure that was not the case. McNabb dropped back and sent a pass down the middle of the field. Mitchell split two defenders for a 28-yard gain, just enough to keep the drive alive.

From there, the Eagles managed a 37-yard David Akers field goal to force overtime. In the extra period,

McNabb throws a touchdown pass against the Packers.

> ## "I just tried to get into a position where Freddie could compete for it. It was just a great play by Freddie."
>
> **—Donovan McNabb**

the Eagles produced a 20–17 victory on another field goal by Akers, this one from 31 yards.

On a day when McNabb became the first quarterback to ever rush for more than 100 yards in a NFL playoff game, one play stood out. The tying and winning field goals by Akers finished the job, but the McNabb-to-Mitchell connection ranks as one of the most famous plays in the history of the Eagles. The Packers knew exactly what the Eagles had to try to do, but they could not stop McNabb and Mitchell from getting at least 26 yards.

"I just tried to get into a position where Freddie could compete for it," McNabb said. "It was just a great play by Freddie."[1] Mitchell credited McNabb with reading the play perfectly.

The comeback meant that the Eagles would finish their season in the NFC Championship game for the third straight year. They were once again one of the last four teams left in the NFL seeking a championship.

The Packers and the New York Giants saw firsthand during that three-year run how McNabb's toughness in tight games was capable of bringing his team back in apparently desperate circumstances.

FANTASTIC FINISHES

The playoff game with Green Bay came after the 2003 regular season. During that season, McNabb led an 8-play, 65-yard drive on *Monday Night Football* to beat the Packers in the final minute. His 6-yard touchdown pass to Todd Pinkston with 27 seconds left produced a 17–14 victory.

The Giants had been victims of two comeback victories in 2001. Like the Packers, they lost in the spotlight of *Monday Night Football*, then fell to a McNabb-led comeback in a more important game late in the season.

Philadelphia trailed New York, 9–3, at the two-minute warning on *Monday Night Football*. McNabb led the Eagles down the field and hit James Thrash with an 18-yard touchdown pass for a 10–9 victory.

The Eagles had more work to do December 30, 2001. They trailed the Giants, 21–14, with 2:43 left. McNabb's 7-yard touchdown pass to Chad Lewis tied the game and paved the way for a 35-yard field goal by Akers. The field goal gave the Eagles a 24–21 win, which clinched the team's first division title in thirteen years.

2001 NFC PLAYOFFS

Wild-Card

Philadelphia 31, Tampa Bay 9

Green Bay 25, San Francisco 15

Divisional

Philadelphia 33, Chicago 19

St. Louis 45, Green Bay 17

NFC Championship

St. Louis 29, Philadelphia 24

Note: New England 20, St. Louis 17 in Super Bowl

HOMECOMING DAY

During those three seasons—from 2001 through 2003—the Eagles were clearly beginning to feel right at home in the playoffs.

Despite winning the division again in 2001, the Eagles were seeded behind the other two division winners. That meant they had to play a game in the wild-card round, and they would have to play on the road the next week. The Eagles defeated the Tampa Bay Buccaneers easily, 31–9, to earn McNabb a special road trip.

McNabb got the chance to return to Chicago and play at Soldier Field for the first time since the 1993 city high school championship game. He made the most of the opportunity, leading a 33–19 win against the Bears. McNabb had a hand in 3 touchdowns. He passed for 262 yards and 2 scores while running for 37 yards and another touchdown.

RUNNING START

McNabb's passing was clearly established, but he was running better than ever when the 2002 season began. He ran for more than 100 yards twice, making him the

DONOVAN MCNABB'S 2001–04 PLAYOFF STATISTICS

vs. Tampa Bay, 2001–02 season: 16-for-25, 194 yards, 2 TDs, 1 interception; 4-for-57 rushing

vs. Chicago, 2001–02 season: 26-for-40, 262 yards, 2 TDs, 1 interception; 8-for-37, 1 TD rushing

vs. St. Louis, 2001–02 season: 18-for-30, 171 yards, 1 TD, 1 interception; 4-for-26, 1 TD rushing

vs. Tampa Bay 2002–03 season: 26-for-49, 243 yards, 1 interception; 3-for-17 rushing

vs. Atlanta, 2002–03 season: 20-for-30, 247 yards, 1 TD; 4-for-24 rushing

vs. Green Bay, 2003–04 season: 21-for-39, 248 yards, 2 TDs; 11-for-107 rushing

vs. Carolina, 2003–04 season: 10-for-22, 100 yards, 3 interceptions; 2-for-10 rushing

first quarterback since Bobby Douglass in 1972 to reach that mark twice in the same season. McNabb also ran for touchdowns in four straight games, making him just the fifth quarterback to accomplish that feat, joining Greg Landry (1972), Pat Haden (1976), Jeff Hostetler (1993), and Kordell Stewart (1997).

The running stopped on that memorable November day when McNabb threw four touchdown passes on a broken ankle. "Playing with a broken leg, throwing four touchdowns in an NFL game, that's the stuff that legends are made of," teammate Chad Lewis said.[2]

2002 NFC PLAYOFFS

Wild-Card

   Atlanta 27, Green Bay 7

   San Francisco 39, New York
     Giants 38

Divisional

   Philadelphia 20, Atlanta 6

   Tampa Bay 31, San Francisco 6

NFC Championship

   Tampa Bay 27, Philadelphia 10

Note: Tampa Bay 48, Oakland 21 in Super Bowl

After six weeks off, McNabb returned to lead the Eagles to a playoff win against the Atlanta Falcons.

PERFECT MONTH

The Eagles found surprising struggles when they opened the 2003 season. After being shut out, 17–0, by the Tampa Bay Buccaneers, they lost, 31–10, to the New England Patriots.

When November arrived, the Eagles were heading in the right direction with two straight wins and a 4–3 record. There was still some uncertainty, however, about whether Philadelphia would catch rival Dallas in the NFC East Division. The Cowboys were 5–2 and had already beaten the Eagles.

The Eagles had an entirely different look by the time the month ended. Philadelphia went 5–0 in a month for the only time in team history, putting together the meat of a nine-game winning streak that carried the team to a division title. McNabb was named NFC Player of the Month. He hit 94 of 145 passes for 1,265 yards and 6 touchdowns in November, going 127 passes without an interception at one point. He also ran for 108 yards and one touchdown.

McNabb reacts to throwing a game-winning touchdown.

ANOTHER CLOSE CALL

The Eagles repeated what was becoming a routine. They started the playoffs on a winning note, but they lost in the end, falling one win short of the Super Bowl.

The fourth-and-26 pass to Mitchell was the most memorable play of the playoff win against Green Bay, but the game was filled with special moments. The Eagles were still trailing, 14–7, in the third quarter when McNabb accounted for 109 yards in one scoring drive, making up for sacks and penalties that pushed the team back. The Eagles converted second-and-20 and first-and-20 situations on the 89-yard scoring drive. McNabb had scrambles of 13 and 24 yards to help him to his record rushing day, and he completed 5 of 6 passes for 72 yards.

"He did a great job," Reid said. "He kept firing and did it with confidence and conviction. Keep shooting, and when you're as great as he is, good things will happen. I love watching him."[3]

DID YOU KNOW?

When Donovan McNabb ran for 107 yards in a 20–17 overtime victory against the Green Bay Packers on January 11, 2004, he became the first quarterback to rush for more than 100 yards in an NFL playoff game. Otto Graham of the Cleveland Browns had the old record with 99 yards rushing in a 1950 playoff game.

The Carolina Panthers intercepted McNabb three times a week later and eventually knocked him out of the game in a 14–3 victory. McNabb suffered a rib injury early in the game and played as long as he could before coming out in the second half. The Eagles trailed 7–3 late in the third quarter, but they again walked away from the NFC Championship game disappointed.

CHAPTER SEVEN

Building a Public Image

Number "5" Philadelphia Eagles jerseys filled the NovaCare practice facility in Philadelphia. While players ages eleven to fourteen ran through a series of football drills on the Eagles' practice field, Donovan McNabb, the reason they were all there—and the reason they all were honored to wear jerseys adorned with the number "5"—walked among them.

The fourth annual All-Star Kids Football Clinic, held June 10, 2006, in Philadelphia, was part of a Philly Flavor Weekend full of events that the Donovan McNabb Foundation runs in an effort to raise money for American Diabetes Association (ADA) programs. McNabb was one of many pro football players the kids interacted with while learning more about the game.

"I enjoy having an opportunity to come out here with the kids and then these guys that we compete every Sunday with, and to have guys like Hall of Fame running back Eric Dickerson here, it's a blast for me," McNabb said. "You want all the kids to meet and greet new guys."[1]

There are some new players mixed with some regulars whom McNabb can count on to help in community events. "I've been coming here for the last three years and the longer I've come, the bigger the crowd," said Eagles teammate Todd Pinkston, who was there working on wide receiver drills.

> **DID YOU KNOW?**
> Diabetes is a chronic metabolic disorder caused by inadequate production of insulin, a hormone produced in the pancreas that allows the body to use and store glucose. Elevated sugar levels in the urine and blood lead to excessive urination, thirst, hunger, weakness, weight loss, and itching. Diabetes can lead to serious vision and cardiovascular problems.

"It's great for not only Donovan, but all these kids."[2]

Brian Westbrook, another Eagle, worked with Dickerson on a station about playing running back. "They're learning the game of football from a young age, and they have the professionals to help them with it," Westbrook said. "We're a team here. Anytime you get a chance to help the community out, it's really all about the kids. I love to help Donovan out anytime I can, but I love to help the kids a lot more."[3]

McNabb is able to recruit the help of teammates because he has built a reputation for a lasting commitment, particularly to the ADA. "First you have to focus on the cause and that's to raise money to help find a cure," he said. "And after that, let's buckle down and have some fun."[4]

AMERICAN DIABETES ASSOCIATION MISSION STATEMENT:
To prevent and cure diabetes and to improve the lives of all people affected by diabetes.

Sam McNabb, Donovan's father and the man most responsible for inspiring him to work with diabetes programs, helps organize the event while Donovan and the other professional football players take an active role in the workouts. As Sam watches, he says the players are showing that they "are kids at heart anyways. They fit right in."[5]

Sam knows firsthand about diabetes. He has type 2 diabetes and is one of 15 million Americans dealing with the disease. It is estimated that another 5 million people may have the disease and be unaware of it.

"Awareness is the only way we are going to fight diabetes," he said. "The goal of our foundation is to save the lives of children and adults living with the disease through education, exercise, diet control, and regular check-ups by a doctor."[6]

McNabb and his mother, Wilma, participate in a competition sponsored by Campbell's Chunky Soup.

McNabb's style of play, combining flashy skill and stunning toughness, made him one of the most recognizable players in the NFL. That recognition led to commercials and helped McNabb's image grow away from the field. Along with his parents, McNabb was part of television commercials that made his face more recognizable by taking him out from under his football helmet. In Philadelphia, the public has seen an even more impressive image. McNabb's community and charitable involvement pay back the city that has rallied around its star quarterback.

Involvement with organizations such as the ADA spreads McNabb's contributions to people all across the country. Part of the money raised in the Philadelphia area is used for national programs.

"It is through events like 'Philly Flavor' that the foundation is able to fund diabetes research," McNabb said. "It is a never-ending fight. We have made progress, but there is still a lot of work that needs to be done."[7]

McNabb's family is right there with him for that work. His mother, Wilma, is the executive director of the Donovan McNabb Foundation and runs McNabb Unlimited, which oversees McNabb's endorsement deals. McNabb's father and his brother, Sean, are also involved in many of his projects.

The McNabb family as a whole was honored by the ADA. "It is impossible to measure what the McNabb family has done for people with diabetes and ADA's camping program," said Susan Yannessa, executive director of ADA's central Pennsylvania and southern New Jersey area. "The

**DID YOU KNOW?
DONOVAN MCNABB'S FAMILY**

**Wife: Raquel Nurse
    (married June 2003)**

**Daughter: Alexis
    (born September 2004)**

Father: Samuel

Mother: Wilma

Brother: Sean

McNabbs continue to increase their involvement and commitment, which the American Diabetes Association recognized this year with the renaming of our camping program to the Donovan McNabb Diabetes Camp for Kids. Their ongoing financial commitment helps ensure a bright future for the hundreds of children that attend our camps every summer."[8]

Diabetes is the main concentration, but McNabb has other public and charitable interests. He can be seen away from the football field, playing in charity basketball games, making appearances at schools in the Philadelphia area, and making major donations to his former schools, Mount Carmel High School in Chicago and Syracuse University. McNabb also brings Christmas presents to community centers to help selected needy families each year.

> **DID YOU KNOW?**
> Information about camping programs for children with diabetes can be obtained by calling 1-800-342-2383.

When the NFL did its part to try to help with Hurricane Katrina efforts, McNabb was in New York, working the phones during a relief fund telethon. "For me to be part of it, first and foremost, was something special," McNabb said. "I was asked to come down and to just encourage the fans and everyone to help donate, or just lend a hand. Without second-guessing I said that I would be there." Once there, McNabb was impressed with the amount of help pouring in from around the country. "To get down there and answer the phones, I've never seen a phone ring so fast; as soon as you put it down," he said. "To see the amount of money that we raised while we were there just picking up the phone says a lot about the people across this country."[9]

People all across the country seem to respond to McNabb's personality. That is why so many companies seek to have him endorse their products. Reebok is introducing a Donovan McNabb clothing line.

"All of the things off the field are just a dream come true and what I'm doing now is reality, playing football," McNabb said. "All of the things off the field come from your success on the field."[10]

McNabb has done promotional work for the Lincoln Financial Group, which purchased naming rights to Lincoln Financial Field, where the Eagles play their home games. He has worked with Reebok and Pepsi. McNabb was part of the national ad campaign for DirectTV's NFL packages and shot commercials for the NFL's Youth Program.

The ongoing relationship with Campbell's Soup, in a series of commercials since 2001, has made Wilma McNabb a star. Wilma is often recognized on the street as the "Campbell's Soup Mom." McNabb is happy he is able to share so much of his success with his parents.

Wilma McNabb talks about the first Chunky Chili Bowl event to raise awareness about hunger in the United States.

"I'm very close to my parents," he said. "Fortunately for me, I had two parents in the household who continued to stress discipline, who continued to stress that I had to be the hardest worker to achieve anything. . . . These are two people I honor and cherish. They're a major part of my life, as well as my wife and my daughter."[11]

CHAPTER EIGHT

Super Bowl Bound

Donovan McNabb stood on the field at the Edwards Jones Dome in St. Louis following his first National Football Conference Championship game loss in January 2002. McNabb watched the Rams celebrate their NFC title and the prize that went with it—a trip to the Super Bowl. McNabb sought motivation and important lessons in watching another team celebrate a goal that he and his Eagles teammates pursued so fiercely.

The Eagles came up a game short each of the next two years, but McNabb did not have time to observe another team celebrating. He was busy tending to injuries to his ankle and ribs after those games.

Finally, in January of 2005, on the fourth straight chance, the Eagles broke through. They earned a berth in the Super Bowl and moved within one win of the ultimate goal of each professional football player. As the Rams players had done three years earlier, McNabb was able to share that moment with his home fans.

TEAMS WITH FOUR OR MORE CONSECUTIVE CONFERENCE CHAMPIONSHIP GAME APPEARANCES

Team	Seasons	Record
Oakland	1973–77	1–4
Buffalo	1990–93	4–0
Dallas	1992–95	3–1
Dallas	1970–73	2–2
Philadelphia	2001–04	1–3
Oakland	1967–70	1–3

"It's just a great feeling for the city of Philadelphia," McNabb said after a 27–10 victory against the Atlanta Falcons. "Obviously, we know what happened the last three years, this close and never being able to really pull it out. Everything that's happened so far has been a special feeling and there's no reason to stop now."[1]

There was still work to be done in the future. McNabb knew that was a possibility, even while

McNabb signals to the sidelines during the 2005 NFC Championship game.

celebrating the biggest victory of his professional career. "There's no relief, really, for me," he said during the break between the NFC Championship game and the Super Bowl. "I set a goal to win the Super Bowl and that's where I'm going with it," he said. "Obviously, we're excited about this win and we're excited about winning the NFC Championship and putting ourselves in position to go to the Super Bowl and we're not done. So we are going to enjoy while the time is here and focus in on what we need to do to win the Super Bowl."[2]

The Eagles made it to the Super Bowl but came up short in Jacksonville, Florida. They could not stop the New England Patriots from winning their third championship in four years with a 24–21 victory. McNabb passed for 357 yards and 3 touchdowns, but he also threw 3 interceptions. He led his team to one late touchdown drive in an attempted comeback, but he was criticized by some for not moving the team fast enough to make a second score more likely.

> "... we are going to enjoy while the time is here and focus in on what we need to do to win the Super Bowl."
>
> —Donovan McNabb

HOW TO FIGURE A PASSING RATING

The National Collegiate Athletic Association (NCAA) and National Football League (NFL) each have a passing efficiency ratings formula, which intends to do just as its name implies, rate the efficiency of each passer. The ratings do not attempt to rank running ability or other roles that a quarterback plays in a team's offense. They serve purely as a comparison of passing statistics.

The ratings formulas are different for both organizations. They do, however, have two similarities. Both formulas combine four factors: completion percentage, average yards gained per attempt, touchdown percentage, and interception percentage. They also are based on past established statistics that were used to try to determine an "average" performance.

The NCAA formula, which has no maximum value and technically could produce a negative number, is based on 100.0. If a quarterback is exactly average in all four categories, his rating would be 100.0. The NCAA formula was created in 1979. The average performance was determined by adding the totals of all passers in major college football from 1965 through 1978, a span of fourteen seasons.

McNabb's college passing ratings ranged from a low of 145.1 in his sophomore season to a high of 162.3 as a freshman. They were always well above average.

The NFL formula puts a minimum point total of zero and a maximum of 39 7/12 for each of the four categories. The lowest possible rating is zero. The highest possible rating is 158.3. A rating of 66.7 is considered average. The NFL formula was created in 1971, based on average statistics from the 1970 season.

McNabb's NFL passing ratings have been at 77.8 or higher since his first full season as a starter. He had a 60.1 rating as a part-time starter in his rookie season. He has been higher than 80 in four of his last five seasons, including a career-high 104.7 in the Super Bowl season of 2004.

Rules have changed slightly, and passing games have improved since the time when the formulas were created. Therefore, the average modern quarterback has a rating slightly higher than 100.0 in college and 66.7 in the NFL. Still, McNabb's career marks of 155.1 and 84.1 rank well above average.

McNabb pauses during a press conference in Philadelphia January 17, 2003. The Eagles were preparing for the Super Bowl.

The Eagles and McNabb left Super Bowl XXXIX still searching for that one more win to become champions of the NFL. There was no mistaking, however, that they had just been through a special season. The Eagles matched the 1980 team as the only ones in team history to reach the Super Bowl. By any individual measurement, it was the best season of McNabb's career. His NFL passing rating, which is 84.1 for his career and was 86.0 in his previous best season, soared to 104.7. He passed for 3,875 yards, eclipsing his previous seasons' totals by more than

500 yards. He also became the first NFL quarterback to throw for more than 30 touchdowns while throwing fewer than 10 interceptions. He finished with 31 touchdown passes and just 8 interceptions.

NEW COMBINATION

The arrival of Terrell Owens prior to the start of the 2004 season gave McNabb his first chance to run the Philadelphia passing game with the help of one of football's elite receivers. McNabb had always found ways to succeed despite not having a receiver who made opponents alter their defenses.

With Owens now part of the attack, McNabb put up a series of amazing passing numbers.

The potency of the Philadelphia attack was evident right from opening day. The McNabb-to-Owens combination clicked for 3 touchdown passes, including Philadelphia's first two scores of the season. The Eagles started on their way to a 13–3 season with McNabb completing 26 of 36 passes for 330 yards and 4 touchdowns in a 31–17 win against the New York Giants.

McNabb passed for 376 yards and 4 more touchdowns in a 34–31 overtime win against the Cleveland Browns October 24. It was the sixth straight win during a 7–0 start.

With much of the NFL watching on November 15, McNabb had another 300-yard, 4-touchdown effort on *Monday Night Football*. This time, the final yardage total was 345 on just 28 attempts in a 49–21 romp against the Cowboys. Three of the touchdown passes came by the midway point in the second quarter, giving the Eagles a 28–7 lead. A week later, McNabb threw for 4 more touchdowns, but his yardage total was down to 222, because he only needed 26 attempts (and 18 completions) to beat the Washington Redskins, 28–6.

Terrell Owens catches the ball in a game against the Chicago Bears October 3, 2004.

The back-to-back, 4-touchdown games were simply a preview to the most remarkable numbers of McNabb's career.

He finished a 27–6 victory against the Giants on November 28 by hitting the final 10 passes that he attempted. That streak of completions continued until McNabb had connected on 24 straight passes, breaking the NFL record of 22 set by Hall of Famer Joe Montana during a 2-game stretch in 1987.

The 14 straight completions against Green Bay on December 5 were the start of a game in which McNabb threw 5 touchdown passes in the first half. He finished the day with a team-record 464 yards passing while hitting 32 of 43 attempts. Running back Brian Westbrook, who finished with a remarkable 11 catches for 156 yards, had 3 of the touchdowns as the Eagles took a 35–0 lead with 1:48 left in the second quarter. The Eagles coasted from there for a 47–17 rout.

After the Eagles ran away from the division with a 13–1 start, McNabb threw just 3 passes in the final 2 games while watching many of the

> **DID YOU KNOW?**
>
> The Philadelphia Eagles won more than twice as many games as any other team in the National Football Conference East Division during the 2004 season. The Eagles won the division by 7 games, going 13–3. The New York Giants, Dallas Cowboys, and Washington Redskins all tied for second with 6–10 records.

Philadelphia reserves play in a pair of losses. The 2-game losing streak did not mean a thing, but the Eagles headed to the playoffs without Owens, who suffered a broken bone in his lower leg.

PLAYOFF PROWESS

Clearly, Owens' presence had helped McNabb put up the best passing numbers of his career. But, if the Eagles were going to overcome three years of disappointment, they were going to have to do it without their newest star. Once again, the vast majority of the pressure for Philadelphia's success rested on McNabb's shoulders.

2004 NFC PLAYOFFS

Wild-Card
Minnesota 31, Green Bay 17
St. Louis 27, Seattle 20

Divisional
Atlanta 47, St. Louis 17
Philadelphia 27, Minnesota 14

NFC Championship
Philadelphia 27, Atlanta 10

Note: New England 24, Philadelphia 21 in Super Bowl

DONOVAN MCNABB'S 2004 PLAYOFF STATISTICS

vs. Minnesota: 21-for-33, 286 yards, 2 TDs; 3-for-3 rushing

vs. Atlanta: 17-for-26, 180 yards, 2 TDs; 10-for-32 rushing

vs. New England: 30-for-51, 357 yards, 3 TDs, 3 interceptions; 1-for-0 rushing

McNabb pushes away Minnesota Vikings cornerback Antoine Winfield September 20, 2004, in Philadelphia.

He did not disappoint. McNabb efficiently ran the offense. He hit 38 of 59 passes for 466 yards and 4 touchdowns in playoff wins against the Minnesota Vikings and the Atlanta Falcons.

In the division playoffs against Minnesota, McNabb threw touchdown passes in the first quarter and in the first minute of the second quarter. The Eagles took 14-point leads twice in the first five minutes of the second quarter on the way to a 27–14 win against the Vikings and their fourth straight NFC Championship game appearance.

The Eagles were superb defensively throughout the NFC playoffs, allowing the offense to concentrate on controlling the ball and avoiding turnovers. The Eagles churned out 22 first downs and never turned the ball over against Atlanta. A second-half shutout by the defense and 2 McNabb-to-Chad Lewis touchdown passes produced the comfortable victory.

"It was definitely everything I thought it would be," McNabb said, reflecting on that day in St. Louis when he watched the Rams celebrate. "Obviously, it took a couple of years after that for it to happen, but patience is something else and, you know, we continue to stay patient. We know a lot of people turned their backs on us and just didn't have the confidence that we would be able to do it. I think we answered a lot of questions. I think we answered a lot of critics, so maybe people will be happy about the Philadelphia Eagles."[3]

SUPER BOWL

The Eagles wound up in the closest Super Bowl ever played. Unfortunately, they got into that game with the Patriots, who won their third Super Bowl in four years—all in games decided by three points.

The turnovers that they managed to avoid in the NFC playoffs cost the Eagles in the Super Bowl. They lost the ball twice in New England territory in the first quarter, once on a McNabb interception and another time on a pass that L.J. Smith caught, then fumbled.

Despite the early turnovers, the Eagles scored first. McNabb passed 17 and 40 yards to Todd Pinkston to key an 8-play, 81-yard drive. He then found Smith for a 6-yard touchdown. David Akers added the extra point for a 7–0 lead with 9:55 left in the half.

The Patriots forced a tie by halftime. They scored with 1:10 remaining in the second quarter on a 4-yard pass from Tom Brady to David Givens, and Adam Vinatieri added the extra point.

For just the second time in Super Bowl history, a game was tied at halftime. When each team added a touchdown in the third quarter, the Super Bowl went into the fourth quarter tied for the first time ever. Brady passed 2 yards to Mike Vrabel for New England's score early in the third, and McNabb passed 10 yards to Westbrook for Philadelphia's score later in the quarter.

New England took command early in the fourth quarter. Corey Dillon's 2-yard run completed a 9-play, 66-yard drive for a 21–14 lead with 13:44 left. Vinatieri kicked a 22-yard field goal with 8:40 remaining for a 10-point lead.

McNabb is chased by New England Patriots linebacker Rosevelt Colvin in the first quarter of Super Bowl XXXIX.

The Eagles had to score on their next possession no matter what. It also would help to use as little time as possible. McNabb repeatedly worked his team out of trouble, but it took time. He completed two short passes to Owens to convert third-down situations in Philadelphia territory. McNabb then found Freddie Mitchell for 11 yards on a third-and-10 from the New England 30.

"It is definitely everything I thought it would be."

—Donovan McNabb

There was little time for patience. After almost four minutes, the Eagles completed a 13-play, 79-yard drive when McNabb passed the final 30 yards to Greg Lewis with 1:48 left. Akers added the kick to cut the New England lead to 24-21.

With the two-minute warning already gone, Eagles coach Andy Reid decided he needed to try an on-side kick to try to get the ball right back. The gamble failed. But the Eagles' defense held, forcing a punt.

After the short kickoff, the resulting field position allowed New England to pin Philadelphia at its 4-yard line with a punt. With 96 yards to cover in 46 seconds, McNabb tried to remain patient. He slipped a short pass over the middle to Westbrook, but it managed just 1 yard, and time was running out. One last attempt to throw the ball down the field resulted in McNabb's third interception on a day that he threw for 357 yards. Rodney Harrison's second interception of the game allowed New England to celebrate another close victory.

"Three interceptions. I don't look at the touchdowns," McNabb said. "As the quarterback, you want to make sure you take care of the ball. Turnovers kill you and they hurt us today."[4]

Injuries and Insults

Donovan McNabb entered the 2005 season coming off 5 straight Pro Bowls and 4 straight trips to the National Football Conference Championship game. There was no way of guessing that the year following the Super Bowl would turn out to be the most trying of his athletic career.

McNabb tried playing through injuries again, but that was just the start of his problems. Wide receiver Terrell Owens began criticizing McNabb following the Super Bowl and kept up the public attack before the Eagles eventually removed him from their active roster. It was not long before McNabb was inactive as well, giving in to his doctor's recommendations and ending his season early to have surgery for a sports hernia.

"If I can avoid it, I definitely will avoid it."

—Donovan McNabb said of surgery

Owens had come back from a broken ankle that required surgery, returning just seven weeks after the injury to play for the Eagles in the Super Bowl. McNabb connected with Owens 9 times for 122 yards in the game, but Owens was highly critical of the team's established leader. As Owens debated with Eagles management about his contract and other issues, he often made McNabb part of the public debate. He seemed bothered by McNabb's lucrative contract and hinted that McNabb should have supported his fight for a better contract.

The Eagles eventually reached the point where they decided to sit Owens down. They proceeded with McNabb leading the offense as usual, but he was facing more than just the loss of his most talented receiver. McNabb was trying to play with a painful injury that got worse as it was aggravated several times during the season.

When his abdominal injury was diagnosed as a sports hernia, McNabb heard speculation that he could not make it through the demands of a long NFL season with such a painful injury. McNabb, however, was determined to try. The Eagles were off to a 3–1 start, and recent history made them division favorites.

VOLATILE SUBJECT

The number of African-Americans playing quarterback for major college and professional teams is constantly on the rise.

There was a day when some coaches hesitated to use talented African-American players at quarterback, pushing them to other positions. Clearly, the subject still brings out controversial debate.

During a brief stint as a commentator on ESPN's Sunday NFL Countdown, conservative national talk show host Rush Limbaugh questioned whether Donovan McNabb's race was causing him to be protected from criticism.

"I think what we've had here is a little social concern in the NFL," Limbaugh said. "The media has been very desirous that a black quarterback do well. There is a little hope invested in McNabb, and he got a lot of credit for the performance of this team that he didn't deserve."

J. Whyatt Mondesire, the president of the Philadelphia branch of the National Association for the Advancement of Colored People (NAACP), offered the opinion that McNabb was not being true to his race when he gradually cut down on the amount of running he did as a quarterback. Mondesire wrote in a newspaper column that McNabb was trying too hard to avoid the racial stereotype that African-American quarterbacks have the tendency to want to run too much. He wrote that McNabb's change in style amounts to "a breach in faith but also belittles the real struggles of black athletes who've had to overcome real racial stereotypecasting."

ESPN management called Limbaugh's comments "insensitive and inappropriate," and Limbaugh resigned less than a week later.

Mondesire's comments triggered more debate on the sensitive subject.

It is tough for some to understand how McNabb keeps winding up as the subject of such criticism. "It baffles me how a guy who does everything right, who goes about his business the way he does, continues to find himself in the eye of the storm," FOX Sports analyst Troy Aikman, a former Dallas Cowboys quarterback, said. "That's just mind-boggling to me."

McNabb drops back in the pocket against Dallas.

The Eagles were one of the top contenders for a Super Bowl title. McNabb brushed aside suggestions of surgery in a late September interview.

"If I can avoid it, I definitely will avoid it," he said. "If that's the case that I have to have it, then it will happen."[1]

More than ever, McNabb needed help from the rest of the Philadelphia offense to make his task more manageable. Unfortunately, the Eagles now lacked a big-play receiver, and their running game was struggling. Other injuries put even more pressure for offense on McNabb.

WHAT IS A SPORTS HERNIA?

A sports hernia is a general term describing a variety of injuries involving tears in muscles of the lower abdomen. The tear can lead to the muscle pulling away from bones. The process of twisting and bending over while under force, such as a high-speed hit in football, can cause tears in abdominal muscles.

The symptoms of a sports hernia include pain in the lower abdomen, down into the groin. Because the pain can increase with sudden movements, mobility is impaired.

Rest for an extended period of time is usually the first choice to treat a sports hernia. If rest does not allow healing, or if the injury becomes more severe, surgery may be necessary.

Following surgery, physical therapy is needed to regain strength and flexibility in the abdomen and the pelvic area.

AMONG THE LEADERS

Donovan McNabb had thrown more passes (357) than anyone in the NFL for the 2005 season at the time he was injured. At that time, he also ranked second in the league in completions (211) and passing yards (2,507) and tied for third in touchdown passes (16).

The Eagles were pounded by their division rival the Dallas Cowboys, 33–10, but after a week off for a bye, they came back to beat a strong San Diego Chargers team, 20–17, to improve to 4–2. Clearly, they were still in contention.

There were signs of trouble, however, in the win against the Chargers. The Eagles pulled out the victory with 2:25 left when San Diego attempted a field goal to extend its lead to 7 points. Instead, the Eagles blocked the kick, and Matt Ware returned it 65 yards for the winning touchdown.

The Eagles needed the special teams heroics. Their offense had been struggling. McNabb, despite his injuries, was called on for 61 of the team's 71 offensive plays. He threw 54 passes, was sacked 3 times, and ran 4 times. Brian Westbrook carried on the other 10 plays, but he was ineffective, gaining just 25 yards. McNabb, unable to move as well as normal, was the target on more hits than just the 3 sacks. The Chargers drove him to the ground after he threw passes on 2 occasions, drawing roughing-the-passer penalties. The chances to go after McNabb were plentiful. With the running game sputtering, the Eagles threw passes on 25 straight offensive plays at one point in the game. The same offensive line that was having trouble opening holes for the running game was faced with the difficult task of holding back opposing pass rushes, which now included an increasing number of blitz packages.

As it turned out, McNabb would not take part in another winning game all season. He struggled through 3 straight losses. In his last game, the ground game came around to produce 181 yards, and McNabb even ran for a score. The Eagles held a late lead against the Cowboys, but McNabb threw an interception, then hurt himself trying desperately to make a tackle on the touchdown return that gave Dallas a 21–20 victory.

After his fall on the interception, McNabb was having more serious pain in his groin as well. There was no more avoiding the fact that the sports hernia needed surgery.

LOWEST CAREER INTERCEPTION PERCENTAGE AMONG ACTIVE NFL QUARTERBACKS (THROUGH END OF 2005 SEASON)	
Donovan McNabb	2.24
Mark Brunell	2.35
Jeff Garcia	2.59
Tom Brady	2.59
Steve McNair	2.66

"I'm disappointed that the injury has reached this stage and has ultimately ended my season."

—Donovan McNabb

"I'm disappointed that the injury has reached this stage and has ultimately ended my season," McNabb said in a prepared statement. "I wanted so much to help this team turn it around and was unable to do that."[2]

McNabb had started 37 of the previous 38 games, missing only the 2004 regular-season finale while resting for the playoffs. He had missed only 7 games because of injury in 6 seasons, with 6 of those coming after his broken ankle.

The sports hernia injury meant that for one of the few times in his career, McNabb was not able to come up with a way to lead the Eagles to bigger and better performances.

CHAPTER TEN

On the Way Back

Andy Reid had just been appointed head coach of an NFL team for the first time in his career. The first major decision in the biggest job of Reid's life was who to choose with the second overall pick in the 1999 NFL Draft.

Despite contrary opinions elsewhere, Reid trusted Donovan McNabb to be that first selection. Less than a year later, Reid trusted McNabb with the most important position on a football team, the job of starting quarterback.

After the 2005 season, he was again counting on McNabb to lead the way as the 2006 season approached. Seven years earlier, Reid trusted his instincts and his evaluation of what type of

McNabb and head coach
Andy Reid watch practice.

professional football player McNabb could become. His more recent decisions are based on proof of what McNabb can do for an NFL team and has done for the Philadelphia Eagles franchise.

McNabb's body—and to a lesser extent, his image—needed healing after the 2005 season. For the most part, McNabb handled the delicate balance of the Terrell Owens controversy well. He defended himself when he thought it was necessary, but he tried to avoid being part of a constant public debate. In addition, the muscles of his abdomen needed time to rest following surgery. By the time off-season public appearances and mini-camps rolled around, McNabb was back out trying to re-establish himself and the Eagles as threats to remain among the best in the NFL.

Reid and the rest of the Eagles management had already made it clear that McNabb was the man to lead their team. When Owens' many complaints included personal attacks that challenged McNabb's role as the team leader, it became clear that it would be tough for the team to move forward with both players. One had to go, but one needed to be kept to build the offense around.

"Donovan's got a knack for leading people."

—Jon Runyan

"Donovan's got a knack for leading people," Eagles tackle Jon Runyan said. "He handles things the way you want your quarterback

McNabb participates in football camp July 26, 2006.

to, with confidence. The young guys look to that and they feed off of it. The veterans feed off of it, too. This offense is going to go where he takes us."[1]

As he had done in that first coaching move, Reid chose McNabb. The Eagles would rebuild around the same man whom Reid originally built his powerhouse around.

COMEBACK KID

Donovan McNabb seems to keep cool when the pressure should be at its most intense. He has helped the Eagles pull out a series of wins in the fourth quarter and overtime during his career.

Here is a list of the top 10 victories in which McNabb has helped the Eagles' offense produce the winning points in the final two minutes of regulation or in overtime:

1. January 20, 2004: The Eagles take over with 2:21 left, trailing by 3 in their NFC Divisional Playoff game with the Green Bay Packers. McNabb completes a fourth-and-26 pass to Freddie Mitchell for a first down, leading to a game-tying field goal by David Akers. The Eagles move again in overtime, and Akers adds the winning field goal in a 20–17 victory.

2. December 30, 2001: The Eagles are behind, 21–14, with 2:43 remaining. McNabb leads 2 scoring drives, throwing a 7-yard touchdown pass to Chad Lewis and setting up a game-winning, 35-yard field goal by Akers to beat the New York Giants, 24–21, and clinch the team's first NFC East Division title in 13 years.

3. November 12, 2000: McNabb hits 12 of 18 passes for 106 yards and a touchdown during the fourth quarter and overtime. He leads the Eagles, who trailed Pittsburgh, 23–13, with less than 3 minutes remaining, to a 26–23 overtime victory.

4. November 10, 2003: The Eagles drive 65 yards in 8 plays during the final three minutes to score on McNabb's 6-yard pass to Todd Pinkston in a 17–14 win against the Green Bay Packers.

5. November 26, 2000: McNabb's career-long, 54-yard run sets up the winning field goal in a 23–20 victory against Washington.

6. September 25, 2005: After Oakland ties the game with 2:17 left, McNabb hits 4 passes of more than 10 yards, including a 13-yarder to Greg Lewis on third-and-nine to set up a 23-yard field goal by Akers with nine seconds left in a 23–20 win.

7. October 22, 2001: McNabb finds James Thrash with an 18-yard pass for the team's only touchdown in the final two minutes of a 10–9 victory against the New York Giants.

8. October 24, 2004: McNabb's 28-yard scramble sets up a 50-yard field goal by Akers in overtime for a 34–31 victory against the Cleveland Browns.

9. December 19, 2004: Two plays after McNabb hits Brian Westbrook for 11 yards on third-and-nine, Dorsey Levens scores on a 2-yard run to pull out a 12–7 victory against the Dallas Cowboys.

10. November 5, 2000: McNabb leads a two-minute drive to force overtime, and then helps set up the winning field goal in a 16–13 victory against Dallas.

McNabb rolls out to pass during the Eagles' football camp in Bethlehem, Pennsylvania, July 25, 2006.

REASONABLE CHOICE

There were many reasons for McNabb to have the trust of the Eagles. Although not directly related to football performance, his status in the community showed the type of character an organization likes to have in a person it builds around. McNabb is able to provide leadership beyond calling the plays in the huddle and finding which players to get the ball to once he receives the snap from center.

WINNING COMBINATION

Through the 2005 season, Andy Reid and Donovan McNabb ranked as the sixth-most successful combination of coach and quarterback in the NFL since 1970.

COACH	QUARTERBACK	TEAM	RECORD	PERCENTAGE
John Madden	Ken Stabler	Oakland Raiders	60–19–1	.756
Bill Belichick	Tom Brady	New England Patriots	58–20	.744
Tom Landry	Roger Staubach	Dallas Cowboys	84–29	.743
George Seifert	Steve Young	San Francisco 49ers	62–23	.729
Bud Grant	Fran Tarkenton	Minnesota Vikings	64–27–2	.699
Andy Reid	Donovan McNabb	Philadelphia Eagles	60–28	.682

Reid says McNabb has the right mentality to be quarterback in a high-pressure city on a team with high expectations. "You have to be wired the right way, and Donovan is," the coach said. "When you are in his position, you're going to be presented with a lot of things. There is a certain focus there, so you have to be able to allow so much to roll off your back and tune in to the job at hand. Donovan does that as well as any quarterback I've been around."[2]

PRIME-TIME PERFORMER

McNabb has started in eleven *Monday Night Football* games during his career. During those games, he has thrown for 2,168 yards and 15 touchdowns while running for 6 more scores. The Eagles are 8-3 in those games.

With the football in his hands, McNabb has made the Eagles' offense go. That was especially true in the second half of the 2003 season and throughout the 2004 season. McNabb, who has completed 58 percent of his passes for his career, hit 64 percent for the final 10 games of 2003 and for the entire 2004 season. His passing rating was 98.5 for the last 10 games of 2003 before soaring to 104.7 for 2004.

McNabb has done all of that while maintaining the playfulness that once made coaches and teachers worry whether a young boy knew how to be serious. That style is appreciated by teammate Chad Lewis, a tight end who is often on the receiving end of McNabb's passes.

"There's way more to leadership," Lewis said. "It's his family, the way he treats other people, the way he makes the game fun. If he picks up a blitzing linebacker, he'll smile at him. He's having fun. When he's at his best, he's smiling, laughing, making plays, keeping other people light, and guys rally around that. I've been amazed over the years that he's been able to

"Everybody has to realize that in order for us to get back to the Super Bowl and win it, we all have to play well together."

—Donovan McNabb

do that in the face of such adversity, but he keeps doing it."[3]

McNabb kept doing that through 5 straight winning seasons, enough to give the Eagles reason to be confident he will do it again when healthy. Making the Eagles' locker room a happy place again is one of McNabb's assignments.

As he watched the 2005 season unravel at the end, he knew the Eagles needed to fix attitudes as much as anything. "The main reason we're not a good team is because we don't play as a team," he said. "Everybody has to realize that in order for us to get back to the Super Bowl and win it, we all have to play well together. You never heard anything like this coming from the Indianapolis Colts. You never heard anything like this coming from the New England Patriots. Baltimore, when they won the Super Bowl, they never had anything like this."[4]

McNabb practices with his teammates.

> **"... I just want them to understand that the guy next to you is counting on you to give all that you have. When they look at me, they know I'm going to give all that I have."**
>
> **—Donovan McNabb**

If any of his teammates had lost confidence in him, McNabb figured the best answer was to put in the work necessary to show he was ready to lead the way again.

"How do you get back a locker room?" he asked, before trying to answer the question himself. "By being yourself. What I have to do is make sure the offense is prepared and come back in the best condition possible; give guys an opportunity to make plays. If it's a divided locker room, I can't be the one to bring everybody together and make some speech like I'm Knute Rockne or something. But when I do bring guys together, I just want them to understand that the guy next to you is counting on you to give all that you have. When they look at me, they know I'm going to give all that I have."[5]

Following surgery, McNabb had to rest long enough to give the sports hernia a chance to begin healing right. By the spring and summer, he was out and about at his usual off-season charitable appearances. Publicly, he was the same guy who had won over the city of Philadelphia. Privately, he was putting in the work to show that he is the same quarterback on the field.

Even with the challenges that his profession creates, McNabb loves his life as a professional football player.

"It really is a dream come true," he said. "As a kid, you're playing ball in the park with your friends, it's the last play in the Super Bowl, and I'm going to complete it for a touchdown. That's the sort of thing that kids always dream about. And for me, those dreams are being lived out. I'm privileged to have had the opportunity."[6]

CAREER STATISTICS

PASSING STATISTICS

Year	Team	G	GS	Att.	Comp.
1999	Philadelphia	12	6	216	106
2000	Philadelphia	12	12	569	300
2001	Philadelphia	12	12	493	285
2002	Philadelphia	10	10	361	211
2003	Philadelphia	16	16	478	275
2004	Philadelphia	15	15	469	300
2005	Philadelphia	9	9	357	211
2006	Philadelphia	10	10	316	80
Total		104	98	3,259	1,898

RUSHING STATISTICS

Year	Team	Att.	Yds.	Avg.	TD
1999	Philadelphia	47	313	6.7	0
2000	Philadelphia	86	629	7.3	6
2001	Philadelphia	82	482	5.9	2
2002	Philadelphia	63	460	7.3	6
2003	Philadelphia	71	355	5.0	3
2004	Philadelphia	41	220	5.4	3
2005	Philadelphia	25	55	2.2	1
2006	Philadelphia	32	212	6.6	3
Total		447	2,726	6.1	24

Pct.	Yds.	TD	Int.	Rating
49.1	948	8	7	60.1
58.0	3,365	21	13	77.8
57.8	3,233	25	12	84.3
58.4	2,289	17	6	86.0
57.5	3,216	16	11	79.6
64.0	3,875	31	8	104.7
59.1	2,507	16	9	85.0
57.0	2,647	18	9	95.5
58.2	22,080	152	72	85.2

KEY:
G=Games
GS=Games Started
Att.=Attempts
Comp.=Completions
Pct.=Percentage
Yds.=Yards
TD=Touchdowns
Int.=Interceptions
Avg.=Average

CAREER ACHIEVEMENTS

- 1990 – Illinois Class 5A state football championship at Mount Carmel High School in Chicago

- 1991 – Illinois Class 5A state football championship at Mount Carmel High School in Chicago

- 1995 – Big East Football Conference Rookie of the Year for Syracuse University

- 1996 – Gator Bowl Most Valuable Player; Big East Football Conference Offensive Player of the Year

- 1997 – Big East Football Conference Offensive Player of the Year

- 1998 – Big East Football Conference Offensive Player of the Year

- 1999 – Second overall selection in National Football League Draft

- 1990s – Big East Football Conference Offensive Player of the Decade

- 2000 – Runner-up in NFL Most Valuable Player voting

- 2004 – Set NFL record by completing 24 straight passes over two games

- 2005 – Starting quarterback for Philadelphia Eagles in Super Bowl XXXIX

CHAPTER NOTES

CHAPTER 1. PLAYING THROUGH THE PAIN

1. Associated Press story on nfl.com, "Eagles win big, but lose McNabb," November 17, 2002, <http://www.nfl.com/gamecenter/recap/NFL_20021117_ARI@PHI> (May 20, 2006).

2. Sal Paolantonio, "Reid questioned for not pulling McNabb," espn.com, November 17, 2002, <espn.go.com/nfl/columns/paolantonio_al/1462641.html> (May 20, 2006).

3. Associated Press story on The Official Site of Donovan McNabb, "McNabb Hopes To Play Through Pain," September 28, 2005, <http://www.donovanmcnabb.com/news/fullstory.php?nid=48&type=news> (May 20, 2006).

4. Ibid.

5. Ibid.

6. "McNabb To Undergo Surgery For Sports Hernia," The Official Site of Donovan McNabb, November 21, 2005, <http://www.donovanmcnabb.com/news/fullstory.php?nid=59&type+news> (June 26, 2006).

7. Ibid.

CHAPTER 2. YOUNG DONOVAN

1. Ray Didinger, "McNabb does it all with a smile," *NFL Insider Magazine*, September–October, 2001 issue, "McNabb does it all with a smile," <http://www.nfl.com/insider/2001/mcnabb_090301.html> (June 7, 2006).

2. Donovan McNabb bio on PhiladelphiaEagles.com, 2005, <http://www.philadelphiaeagles.com/team/teamRosterDetails.jsp?id=195> (May 20, 2006).

3. Anne E. Stein, "Chicago's sports family watches 'Don,'" special to ESPN.com, February 8, 2005, <http://sports.espn.go.com/nfl/playoffs04/news/story?id=1986476> (May 20, 2006).

4. Ray Didinger, "McNabb does it all with a smile," *NFL Insider Magazine*, September–October, 2001 issue, "McNabb does it all with a smile," <http://www.nfl.com/insider/2001/mcnabb_090301.html> (June 7, 2006).

5. Fox Sports Net's "Beyond the Glory," <http://www.suathletics.com/news/basketball/2004/3/12/mcnabbbeyondglory.asp> (June 30, 2006).

6. Coach Paul Pasqualoni's Press Conference Quotes, 2003, <http://www.suathletics.com/Sports/Football/2003/coachpquotesrecruiting.asp> (June 30, 2006).

CHAPTER 3. TWO-SPORT STAR AT SYRACUSE

1. Fox Sports Net's "Beyond the Glory," <http://www.suathletics.com/news/basketball/2004/3/12/mcnabbbeyondglory.asp> (June 30, 2006).

2. Coach Paul Pasqualoni's recruiting quotes, 2004, <http://www.suathletics.com/Sports/Football/2004/coachprecruitquotes> (June 30, 2006).

3. Daryl Gross' remarks at the groundbreaking ceremony, 2005, <http://suathletics.com/Sports/Football/2005/grossquotesnewweightroom05.asp> (June 30, 2006).

CHAPTER 4. DRAFT DAY QUESTIONS

1. By Jim McCabe, "Soaring McNabb gains respect of Eagles fans," *Boston Globe*, February 5, 2005, <http://www.boston.com/sports/football/patriots/articles/2005/02/05/soaring_mcnabb_gains_respect_of_Eagles_fans/> (July 2, 2006).

2. Ibid.

3. Ashley Jude Collie, "His Favorite Play in Philadelphia? The Belly Option," *American Way Magazine*, September 1, 2005, <http://americanwaymag.com/aw/travel/celebrated.asp?archive_date=9/1/2005> (July 7, 2006).

4. Vito Stellino, "Boo! Welcome to Philly, McNabb," *Baltimore Sun*, <http://archive.sportingnews.com/nfl/articles/19990501/154596.html> (July 1, 2006).

5. Fox Sports Net's "Beyond the Glory," <http://www.suathletics.com/news/basketball/2004/3/12/mcnabbbeyondglory.asp> (June 30, 2006).

6. By Jim McCabe, *Boston Globe*, "Soaring McNabb gains respect of Eagles fans," <http://www.boston.com/sports/football/patriots/articles/2005/02/05/soaring_mcnabb_gains_respect_of_Eagles_fans/> (July 2, 2006).

7. Ibid.

8. Ibid.

9. Ibid.

10. Gary Kravitz, "Where are they Now: S Tim Hauck," PhiladelphiaEagles.com, <http://www.philadelphiaeagles.com/news/whereAreTheyNowDetail.jsp?id=28622> (July 1, 2006).

CHAPTER 5. TAKING OVER IN PHILADELPHIA

1. Don Banks, "Eagles QB McNabb remains offense's top option," *NFL Insider*, <http://sportsillustrated.cnn.com/inside_game/don_banks/news/2001/08/16/banks_insider_aug16/> (Accessed July 5, 2006).

2. Ibid.

3. Robert Neely, "Sound bites: Members of the QB Class of '99 speak out," *Pro Football Weekly*, <http://archive.profootballweekly.com/content/archives/draft_1998/draftday_neely1.asp> (July 7, 2006).

4. Gary Kravitz, "Where are they Now: S Tim Hauck," PhiladelphiaEagles.com, <http://www.philadelphiaeagles.com/news/whereAreTheyNowDetail.jsp?id=28622> (July 1, 2006).

CHAPTER 6. KNOCKING ON THE DOOR

1. Associated Press story, January 12, 2004, <http://www.superbowl.com/gamecenter/recap/NFL_20040111_GB@PHI> (July 5, 2006).

2. Fox Sports Net's "Beyond the Glory," <http://www.suathletics.com/news/basketball/2004/3/12/mcnabbbeyondglory.asp> (June 30, 2006).

3. Joanne Korth, *St. Petersburg Times*, "Unbelievable," <http://www.sptimes.com/2004/01/12/Sports/Unbelievable.shtml> (July 3, 2006).

CHAPTER 7. BUILDING A PUBLIC IMAGE

1. Zach Berman, "All Fun For a Good Cause," PhiladelphiaEagles.com, June 10, 2006, <http://www.philadelphiaeagles.com/homeNewsDetail.jsp?id=50060> (July 6, 2006).

2. Ibid.

3. Ibid.

4. Ibid.

5. Ibid.

6. "Father & Son Team Up For Kids," PhiladelphiaEagles.com, June 18, 2005, <http://www.philadelphiaeagles.com/homeNewsDetail.jsp?id=29698> (July 3, 2006).

7. Ibid.

8. American Diabetes Association, <http://www.diabetes.org/communityprograms-and-localevents/africanamericans/celebrity-corner/mcnabb.jsp> (July 3, 2006).

9. Donovan McNabb bio on PhiladelphiaEagles.com, 2005, <http://www.philadelphiaeagles.com/team/teamRosterDetails.jsp?id=195> (May 20, 2006).

10. Donovan McNabb bio on PhiladelphiaEagles.com, 2006, <http://www.philadelphiaeagles.com/team/teamRosterDetails.jsp?id=29780> (July 4, 2006).

11. Les Bowen, "Wilma's son mans fort vs. critics," *Philadelphia Daily News*, June 6, 2006 <http://www.philly.com/mld/philly/sports/football/14749860.htm> (July 3, 2006)

CHAPTER 8. SUPER BOWL BOUND

1. Dave Spadaro, "McNabb Revels In Title Glory," PhiladelphiaEagles.com, January 23, 2005, <http://www.philadelphiaeagles.com/homeNews Detail.jsp?id+22021> (May 20, 2006).

2. Ibid.

3. Ibid.

4. Mike Lopresti, "Another Patriot act: New England dumps Eagles, 24–21," Gannett News Service, *USA Today*, February 6, 2006, <http://www .usatoday.com/sports/scores105/105037/20050206NFL--PHILADELPH0.htm> (July 6, 2006).

CHAPTER 9. INJURIES AND INSULTS

1. Associated Press story on The Official Site of Donovan McNabb, "McNabb Hopes To Play Through Pain," September 28, 2005, <http://www .donovanmcnabb.com/news/fullstory.php?nid=48&type=news> (May 20, 2006).

2. The Official Site of Donovan McNabb, "McNabb To Undergo Surgery For Sports Hernia," November 21, 2005, <http://www.donovanmcnabb.com/ news/fullstory.php?nid=59&type+news> (June 26, 2006).

CHAPTER 10. ON THE WAY BACK

1. Donovan McNabb bio on Philadelphia Eagles Web site, <http://www. philadelphiaeagles.com/team/teamRosterDetails.jsp?id=29780> (August 26, 2006).

2. "A Season That McNabb Won't Soon Forget," The Official Site of Donovan McNabb, November 21, 2005, <http://www.donovanmcnabb.com/news/ fullstory.php?nid=60&type=news> (May 20, 2006).

3. Donovan McNabb bio on Philadelphia Eagles Web site, <http://www .philadelphiaeagles.com/team/teamRosterDetails.jsp?id=29780> (August 26, 2006).

4. Bob Brookover, "McNabb Clears The Air," *Philadelphia Inquirer*, December 11, 2005, <http://www.donovanmcnabb.com/news/fullstory.php? nid=72&type=news> (May 20, 2006).

5. Donovan McNabb bio on Philadelphia Eagles Web site, <http://www. philadelphiaeagles.com/team/teamRosterDetails.jsp?id=29780> (August 26, 2006).

6. Bob Brookover, "McNabb Clears The Air," *Philadelphia Inquirer*, December 11, 2005, <http://www.donovanmcnabb.com/news/fullstory.php?nid= 72&type=news> (May 20, 2006)

GLOSSARY

blitz—A tactic in which the defense uses linebackers or defensive backs to rush the passer.

bowl game—Postseason college football games in which top teams are invited to participate.

charity—The act of giving or an organization that gives to the needy.

diabetes—A chronic metabolic disorder caused by inadequate production of insulin, a hormone produced in the pancreas that allows the body to use and store glucose.

draft—A process in which professional sports teams choose players in order.

efficiency (passing)—Ratings which determine how well quarterbacks pass, by using a formula to combine the major passing statistics.

endorsement—When a celebrity speaks for or makes advertisements about a product in exchange for money.

on-side kick—A strategy in which the team that is kicking off kicks the ball short and tries to recover it before the receiving team takes possession. By rule, the kicking team cannot recover the ball until it has traveled at least 10 yards.

redshirt—The process in which a college athlete sits out a year of competition while studying and practicing. The redshirt year does not count against the four years the player is allowed to compete.

rookie—A first-year professional.

scholarship—A grant of money to a student for educational purposes; top athletes are offered scholarships by colleges to attend and play sports for their schools.

scramble—When a football team plans to pass, but the quarterback winds up running to avoid pass rushers.

FOR MORE INFORMATION

WEB LINKS

Donovan McNabb's official Web site:
www.donovanmcnabb.com

The official site of the National Football League:
www.nfl.com

The official site of the Philadelphia Eagles:
www.philadelphiaeagles.com

Donovan McNabb's page on the Philadelphia Eagles' Web site:
www.philadelphiaeagles.com/team/teamRoster
Details.jsp?id=29780

INDEX

V

W